Mrs. Claus
Takes the Reins

Sue Fliess • illustrated by Mark Chambers

two lions

Published by Two Lions, New York
www.apub.com

Amazon, the Amazon logo, and Two Lions are trademarks of Amazon.com, Inc., or its affiliates.

ISBN-13: 9781503936980
ISBN-10: 1503936988

The illustrations are rendered in digital media.
Book design by Tanya Ross-Hughes

Printed in China
First Edition
10 9 8 7 6 5 4 3 2 1

For my aunt Barbara,
one of the strongest women I know
—S. F.

For the two Christmas elves Elizabeth & Sophie
—M. C.

It's Christmas Eve morning
and everything's set.

So why hasn't Santa Claus woken up yet?

"Santa Claus! Santa Claus! Time to get up!"

"Some hot cocoa, please,
in my jumbo-size cup."

"I'm stuffy. I'm sneezy. I'm slow as a yeti.
My big **ho-ho-ho** isn't holiday ready.

We must cancel Christmas. Oh, what a disgrace!"

"I have a solution . . .
I'll go in your place!"

So Mrs. Claus quickly assembled a crew.

She mapped out a route
from Taiwan to Peru.

She made a supply list
and checked on the weather.

The elves helped her gather
the presents together.

They gave her the list and they packed her some snacks,
then loaded up all of the boxes and sacks.

Then Mrs. Claus bravely climbed onto the sleigh.
"Don't worry," she said.

"I will save Christmas Day!"

With a snap of the reins, she shot into the night.

"Merry Christmas to all!

wish me luck on the flight!"

After some flying, they spied the first town.
She called to the reindeer,

"Let's start
heading down!"

She gracefully shimmied through chimneys with ease,
arranging the presents beneath all the trees.

"This job is so simple.
In fact, it's delightful."

But soon the wind swirled and the weather turned frightful.

She flew through tornadoes, then blizzards and sleet,
which nearly blew Mrs. Claus off of her seat.

The ride became bumpy and things started squeaking.
She saw that the fuel in the sleigh had been leaking!

Keeping her calm as she stayed in control,
she stuffed in some ribbon to plug up the hole.

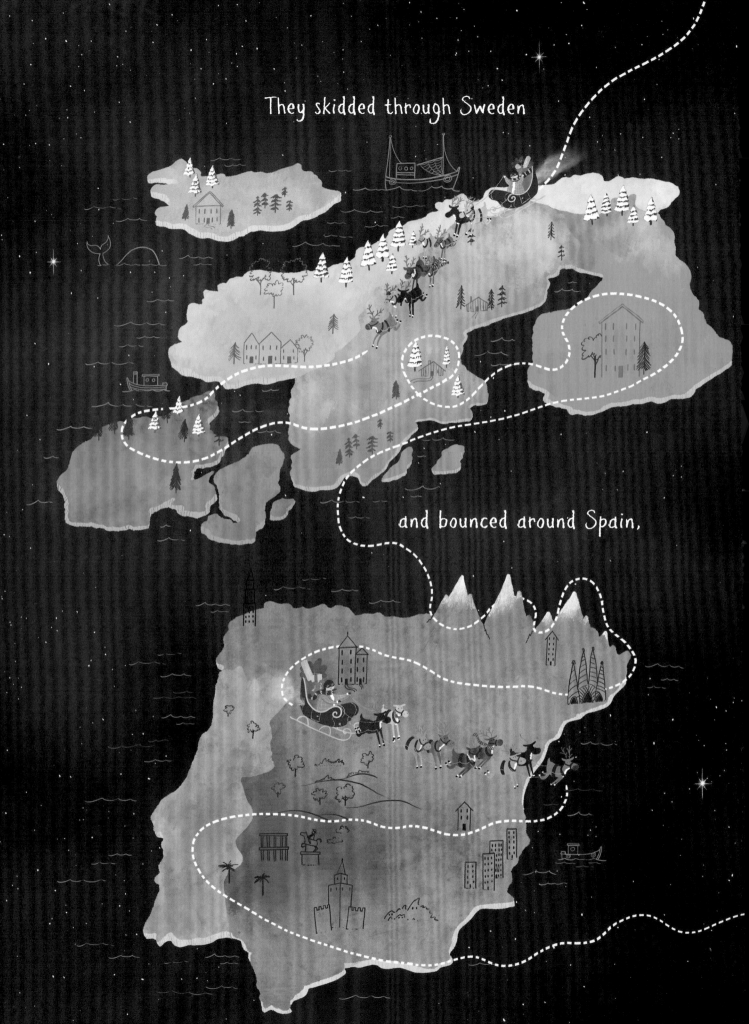

They skidded through Sweden

and bounced around Spain,

then galloped to Texas and zoomed up to Maine.

"Look out!" shouted Rudolph.

"An incoming duck!"

Poor Prancer pulled left
and his bridle got stuck.

A rein became twisted
around Vixen's head,
which made them start traveling
southbound instead!

She had to act fast to untangle the rein.
"I may not have magic, but I've got a brain!"

The problem now conquered, they got back on track.
She felt one more present still left in the sack.

"I'll send it straight down—it's our very last one."
Then Mrs. Claus hollered,

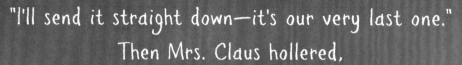

"We're finally done!"

With Rudolph's nose leading the way through the air,
they reached the North Pole with ten minutes to spare.

She entered the workshop and, to her delight,
discovered the elves had been waiting all night.
They lifted her up as they shouted,

"Hooray! Our own Mrs. Claus
has just saved Christmas Day!"